D0478564

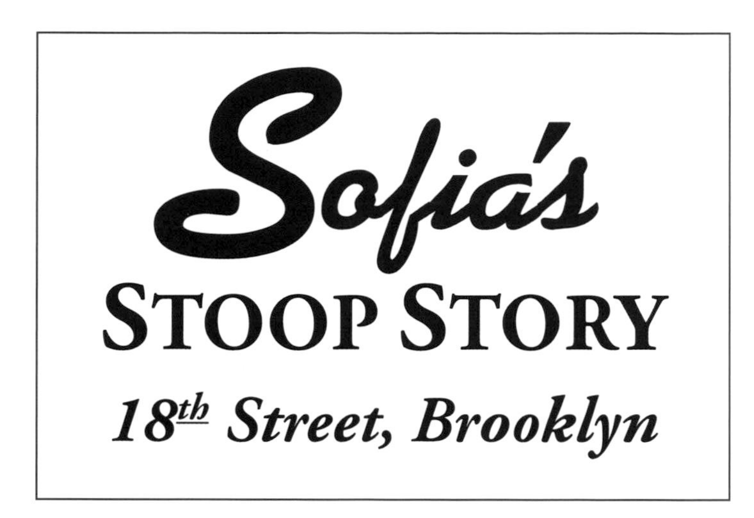
Sofia's
STOOP STORY
18th Street, Brooklyn

In memory of my Uncle Frankie; my Nana;
and my parents, Joe and Marie.
For my sister, Donna; my husband, Glenn;
my children: Erica, Kurt, and Brett;
and my grandson, Dylan, who always loves to hear a good story.
—M.L.B.

For Christy Harris
—S.J. and L.F.

Book layout and design by Steve Johnson and Lou Fancher

Printed and bound in China by Regent Publishing Services, Ltd.
February 2014, Job # 131614

Bohrer, Maria LaPlaca.
Sofia's Stoop Story: 18th Street, Brooklyn / by Maria LaPlaca Bohrer;
illustrations by Lou Fancher & Steve Johnson.
pages cm
ISBN 978-0-9885295-2-6 (alk. paper) ISBN 978-0-98852953-3 (softcover: alk. paper)
[1. Family life--New York (State)--Brooklyn--Fiction. 2. Storytelling--Fiction. 3. Italian Americans--Fiction. 4. Brooklyn (New York, N.Y.)--History--20th century--Fiction.] I. Fancher, Lou, illustrator. II. Johnson, Steve, 1960- illustrator. III. Title.
PZ7.B6358433So 2013
[E]--dc23
2013024421

Blue Marlin Publications
823 Aberdeen Road
West Bay Shore, NY 11706

STOOP STORY

18th Street, Brooklyn

by Maria LaPlaca Bohrer

paintings by Steve Johnson and Lou Fancher

2 lbs.
slices, white br
(crumble and moisten with water
2 cloves of garlic (finely chop
2 eggs (beat in a cup)
1 cup grated Romano cheese
cup of chopped fresh Ital
pinch of salt
pinch of pepper
homemade tomat
olive oil (to fry meatball

I love Sundays. All of my cousins and I spend the day on 18th Street. That's where my Nana lives. And my Uncle Frankie, and my Aunt Emanuela, and my cousin Anna, and my cousin Giuseppe, and my cousin Antonio, and my cousin Arturo, and my cousin Amelia, and my other cousin Amelia, and, well, everyone in the Affisco family. Everyone, except me. I live on Long Island, but on Sundays, 18th Street, Brooklyn is my home.

Uncle Frankie lives next door to Nana. In Brooklyn, the houses are close to each other, so close that sometimes they're connected. And every house has a stoop. Uncle Frankie's stoop is my favorite. It's painted red and white, and there are lots of steps, one for each of my cousins and one for me. There's even a step for Uncle Frankie, but he doesn't sit on it. He sits on an aluminum folding chair. Uncle Frankie says his butt's too old and bony to sit on the stoop. He says when we're as old as he is, we can sit on an aluminum folding chair.

The best part about sitting on Uncle Frankie's stoop is listening to his stories.

"August 14, 1947 was a beautiful day. The guys from the block and I decided to go to a ball game to see one of our favorite players. The Brooklyn Dodgers were playing the Braves at Ebbets Field. But I gotta tell you, this was no ordinary game. This was a game to go down in history for Carl..."

I hear Nana. "Sofia, Sofia viene ca!"

I want to tell Nana, *Not now, Uncle Frankie is telling us a story*, but I know better. When my nana calls, I run.

"Bella mia, go up*a* to Angelini's. I need*a* Romano cheese for my meat-*a*-balls. Make*a* sure he grate*a* for Nana."

"I'll be right back!" I yell to Uncle Frankie as I run up to 6th Avenue.

307
-Specials-
12
EBBETS FIELD
BROOKLYN N.Y.
ALL STAR GAME
UPPER STAND
BOX
74
RAINCHECK
STAR GAME
Dodgers

"Good morning, Mr. Angelini. Nana needs…"

"I know, Sofia. I saved a nice piece of Romano for your nana. Filomena, grate the cheese for Sofia's nana." Mrs. Angelini hands me a small chunk of cheese.

I devour my chunk. I tap the counter top with my fingernails. I tap the wooden floor with my patent leather shoe. How long does it take to grate cheese?

Finally, Mrs. Angelini returns. "Salvatore, the machine doesn't work. Come look!"

"Oh, mamma mia!" Mr. Angelini shouts.

Oh, mamma mia! I want to shout, but I don't.

I hear the hum of the grater. Mrs. Angelini hands me the bag of grated Romano cheese. I hand her the money and race out the door, almost forgetting to say thank you.

The sweet aromas of basil, garlic, and tomatoes reach me two houses before Nana's. Nana makes the best gravy in all of Brooklyn.

"Grazie, grazie, bella mia." Nana leans to kiss my forehead as I drop the bag of cheese on the table and dash to Uncle Frankie's stoop. I plop back down on my step.

Angelini's

“Antonio, do you have ants in your pants?” asks Uncle Frankie. “Giuseppe, stop poking little Amelia! Do you want to hear the rest of the story?” Uncle Frankie asks my cousins.

“Yes, Uncle Frankie.”

“It’s the bottom of the 8th. The game is scoreless. Furillo hits...”

“Carl Furillo?” I ask Uncle Frankie, and then Nana calls me again.

“Sofia, Sofia, viene ca!”

No, no, no! I want to scream, but I know better. I run next door to Nana’s.

“Bella mia, go down*a* to D’Amico’s Bakery*a*, get two loaves o’ Italiano bread*a*, fresh Italiano bread*a*, make sure is*a* fresh. And, we need*a* some cannoli for dessert*a*. Make sure they*a* fresh. Ask Signor D’Amico for the one*a* he made today, not…!”

“I know, Nana. The ones he made today, not yesterday.”

“I’ll be right back!” I yell to Uncle Frankie as I run down to 5th Avenue.

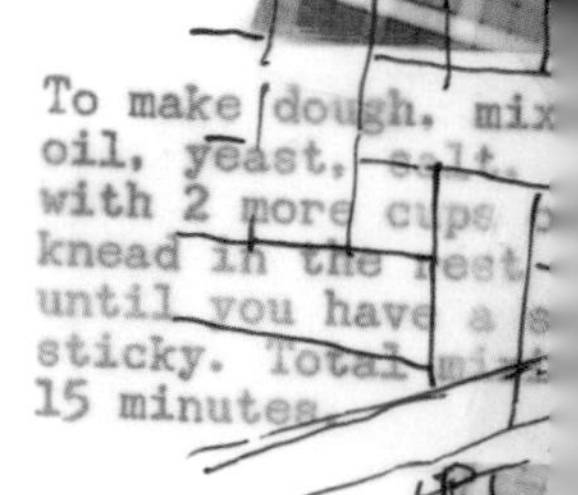

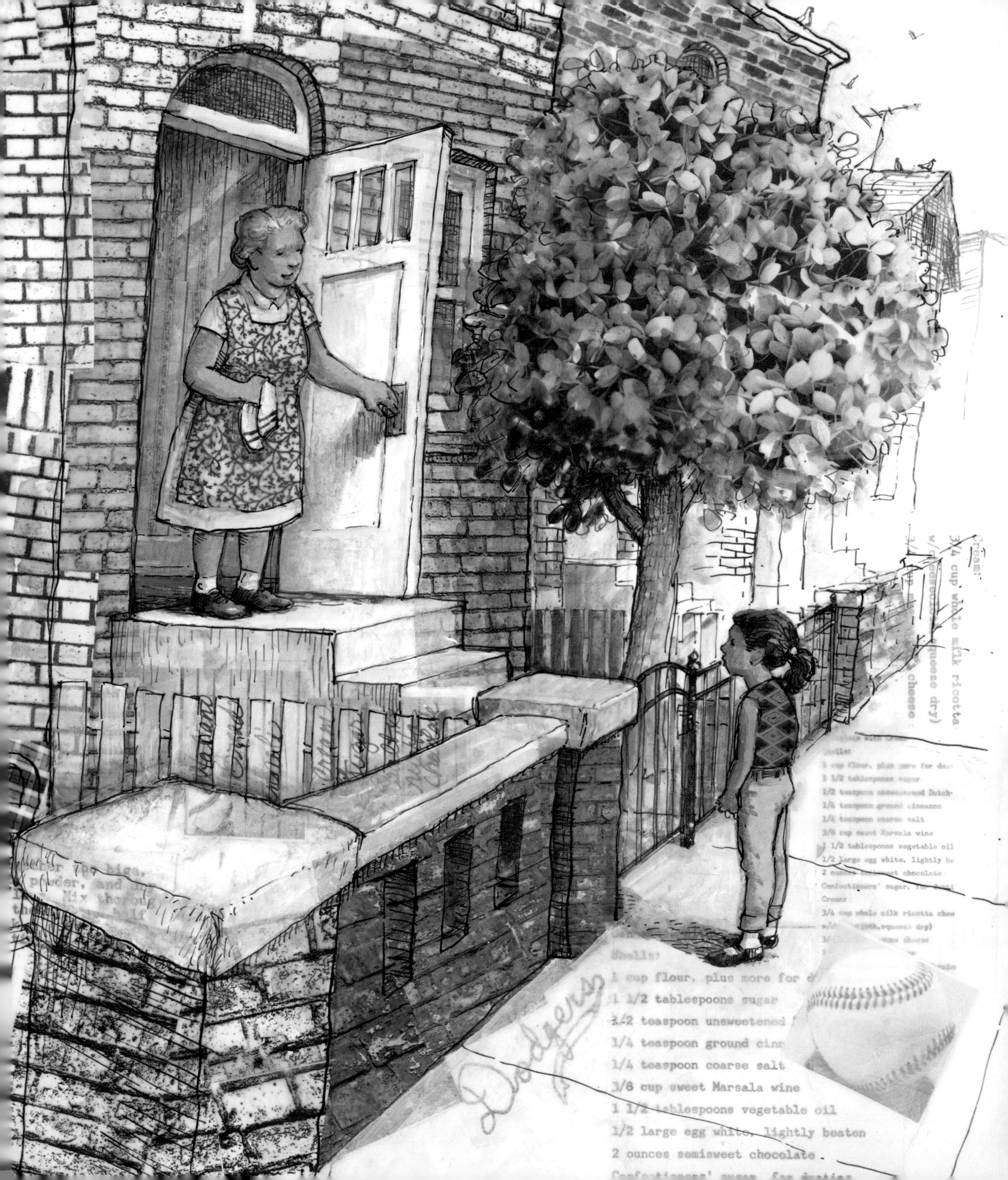
Dodgers
Shells:
1 cup flour, plus more for d
1 1/2 tablespoons sugar
1/2 teaspoon unsweetened
1/4 teaspoon ground cinn
1/4 teaspoon coarse salt
3/8 cup sweet Marsala wine
1 1/2 tablespoons vegetable oil
1/2 large egg white, lightly beaten
2 ounces semisweet chocolate
Cream:
3/4 cup whole milk ricotta

NEW YORK BAY
RY
P
Pampelimossa. Grape fruit.
Pane. Bread.
Pane bianco.
Pane bruno.
bread.
bread.
Pane fresco.
Pane di segala. Rye bread.
Pane abbrustolato. Toast.
Pan pepato.
Panini. Roll.
Patate. Potatoes.
Peperoni
putting loaves in oven.
lightly with water. Bake for 20
Bake them another 20 to 30
BROOK

"Un minuto, Sofia," Mr. D'Amico says as he takes a steaming tray of Italian bread out of the oven. He stuffs two long loaves in a white paper bag. I hug the warm bag, being careful not to squeeze too hard.

"And Nana wants…"

"I know, Sofia, cannoli. But, look here, there's no more left," says Mr. D'Amico.

"Oh…but…but...Nana has to have her cannoli."

Mr. D'Amico winks. "I'm only joking. I saved her some in the back."

"Grazie, grazie, Mr. D'Amico."

When he hands me the cannoli, I ask softly, "Are they…?"

"Yes, Sofia, tell your nana I made them today, not yesterday. Today!"

"Grazie!" I shout as I run out the door.

The aroma oozing from the warm white bag teases me as I race up 18th Street. I can't resist. I tear off a small piece. And then another. And another. By the time I reach Nana's house, only one and a half loaves are left. Nana doesn't mind. Every Sunday, she takes the warm bag of half-eaten bread from me and smiles.

"O sole mio, sta 'n fronte a te!" Nana is singing about her sun again. Before I open the screen door, my nose tells me Nana's frying her meatballs. Nana makes the best meatballs in all of Brooklyn.

Nana's Meatballs
2 lb gr. beef
2 cloves garlic
2 eggs beaten
5 slices bread, wet
1 C Romano
1/4 C parsley
pinch salt, pepper
1/2 C tomato sauce
Ol. oil
- Put meat in bowl
- Make well in center
- add all except oil
- mix, make balls
- brown in oil
- Cool on paper towel
Add to sauce
Mangia

Nana wipes her hands on her apron and sits down. She pats the chair next to her. “Sofia, sit*a* here, next to you Nana.”

“But I want to hear Uncle Frankie’s story, Nana.”

“Oh, you Zio Francesco, he has*a* so many stories to tell.”

“But…,” I try to tell her that this story is special when she gives me *the eye*. So I sit down.

“Sofia, you know I have*a* many grandchildren. Amelia, Anna, Arturo…”

“I know, Nana.”

“But, I have*a* only one Sofia.” She grabs my face and squeezes my cheeks between her hands. “Do you know I am*a* Sofia, too? And when I was*a* you age, I was*a* skinny like*a* you. And my nana feed*a* me meat-*a*-balls, ravioli, braciole, Italiano bread*a*. And then I grow big and strong*a*. Like*a* you cousins.” Nana puts a bowl of meatballs in front of me.

I stuff one meatball in my mouth and stand up.

“Alright*a*, Sofia, you go and hear you zio’s story. But take*a* some meat-*a*-balls wit you.” Nana places three more just-fried meatballs in a paper napkin.

Nana's Meatballs
2 lb gr. beef
2 cloves garlic, chopp
2 eggs, beaten
5 slices bread, broken
wet with water
1 C Grated Romano
1/4 C chopped, fresh parsl
pinch salt & pepper
1/2 C sauce
• put beef in bowl, m
a well
• put all
mix
• make 2 inch balls
• Brown in
• Cool on p
• Mix into
rge bowl, make a well in center
except olive oil and mix
inch balls and place on p
lace meatballs in hot oi
brown
ed meatballs, place on a
wels
to sauce
read
eaten with water)
(finely chopped)
cup)
no cheese
fresh Italian parsle
Focaccia
"Plum" cake
Cream chee
maggio. Cheese
Place ground
Add all ingredients
Shape mixture into
Heat oil, carefull
Neck.
Chuck.
Ribs.
Shoulder clod.
Foreshank.
Brisket.
Cross ribs.

425 degrees.
Dough:
All of the biga
2 cups water

"I can't believe you were at that game! And did you really talk to Carl Furillo, *The Arm*?" asks big Amelia.

"Yes, and I have a keepsake from the day that Carl Furillo called the happiest day of his life." Uncle Frankie closes his eyes. He takes his handkerchief out of his pocket.

"What? You met Carl Furillo? Why was it the happiest day..."

"Venite ca, Sofia, Anna, Giuseppe, Antonio, big Amelia, little Amelia, Arturo, Francesco! Time*a* to mangiar'!" Nana shouts.

Everyone runs to Nana's. Everyone, but me. I sit on my step on Uncle Frankie's stoop.

"Sofia, don't you want to eat?" Uncle Frankie asks.

"I'm not hungry."

"What's wrong, Bella?"

"Everyone else heard your whole story, and I only heard bits and pieces of it. Now, I sit on the stoop to listen to your story, and it's over, *and* we have to go in to eat, *and* I'm not even hungry!"

"Nana," Uncle Frankie yells, "save a dish of ravioli and meatballs for Sofia and me. We'll be in soon."

"Alright*a*, and I save*a* special braciole and a nice*a* sweet sozeech*a* for my Sofia," Nana yells back.

Uncle Frankie sits next to me on my step.

Nana's Meatballs
2 lb gr. beef
2 cloves garlic, chopped
2 eggs, beaten
THANK YOU
STAND
Total $1.25
MAY 13
MAY 3
APR. 24
$3.50
ALL STAR GAME
EBBETS FIELD

“I’ll never forget that day. It was August 14, 1947. My buddies from the block and I decided to go to a ball game to see one of our favorite players, Carl Furillo. The Brooklyn Dodgers were playing the Braves at Ebbets Field. Oh, Sofia, this was no ordinary game. This was a game to go down in history for Carl Furillo. But we didn’t know that then. Before the game, a group of fans presented Furillo with a brand new Buick. Right there on the field! Can you believe that, Sofia? Oh, and we had terrific seats. Boy, were they terrific! We could see every move Furillo made in center field. He played the entire game and didn’t make a single error. Boy, could that guy throw a ball. That’s how he earned the nickname, *The Arm*. And he could hit, too! Picture this, Sofia. It’s the bottom of the 8th. It’s still 0 to 0. Stanky is on second base. Furillo is up at bat. Whack! He hits a line drive deep into left field. Furillo gets a base hit, and Stanky scores! Dodgers 1, Braves 0.” Uncle Frankie sounds like a radio announcer.

6
FURILLO ARRIVES, MIGHTY SLUGGER
Furillo Hits Solo
Furillo's Star
BROOKLYN
Furillo's
WINCHESTER
BATS

Furillo's Star Shines

"Then, top of the 9th, Braves have one out. Furillo catches a fly ball in center field. That's two outs. One more out...game over! Brooklyn Dodgers win 1 to nothing! Furillo drove in the only run that day with a base hit. He got the game-winning RBI! Carl Furillo called that day the happiest day of his life. And the guys and I were there to see it all."

"After the game, my buddies and I hung around the locker room exit, you know, just hanging around and talking about the game. And then, who comes out? Carl Furillo! I couldn't believe my eyes. We ran up to tell him what a great game he played, and we each shook his hand. 'Wait, excuse me, Mr. Furillo,' I called as he started to walk away. I pulled a newspaper from my jacket pocket and asked him to sign his name. 'It would be my pleasure, son,' Mr. Furillo said."

"Did he really say that to you, Uncle Frankie?"

Uncle Frankie puts his hand up. He slowly rises, opens the screen door, and walks into his house. He returns, carrying a neatly folded, yellowed piece of paper. He carefully unfolds the fragile newspaper he's saved since 1947. Written right across the front page of the sports section are the words, *To Frankie, a great Dodgers fan! Carl Furillo.*

Uncle Frankie hands me the yellowed page. "I want you to have this, Sofia. You are a good listener, and a good listener becomes a good storyteller. Someday, Sofia, you will tell this story on my stoop. Or maybe, someday, on your own stoop."

I clutch my signed paper against my chest. My bony butt is starting to hurt. And I don't even care because someday when my butt hurts too much for the stoop, I'll have my very own aluminum folding chair.

BASE BALLS
Furillo Wins Batting
Furillo's Bat Comes Alive
Meatballs
cloves garlic
Mangia!
Put meat in bowl
add all except
oil
brown in oil
Cool on paper

Furillo Hits
Furillo Wins
SLUGGER
16 gr. beef

MBL

Dear Reader,

When I was growing up, Sundays on 18th Street were about Nana's meatballs, gravy, lasagna, braciole, sausage, chicken parmesan, and Italian bread. After the main meal, we ate salad, and finally, dessert: biscotti, cannoli, zeppole, fruit, and an assortment of nuts. However, Sundays were not just about food. They were joyful, fun-filled days spent with family. My sister, my cousins, and I played potsy, caps, and stickball. We sat on stoops and listened to our parents, grandparents, aunts, and uncles tell stories about when they were young. Uncle Frankie's stories about watching Carl Furillo play at Ebbets Field were always our favorites. Oh, how we loved those Sundays together.

Nowadays, I don't spend weekends in Brooklyn, but I carry on the tradition of spending time with my children, grandson, nieces, and nephews. My husband and I live next door to my sister and brother-in-law, but unlike 18th Street, our houses are not connected. And I don't have a stoop, but I do have my mother's aluminum folding chair. That's where I sit when I tell my grandson stories about my Brooklyn Sundays.

Ask your family members to share their stories with you. Listen closely and write them down. Someday, I hope you will tell your treasured stories to someone special, as you sit on your very own aluminum folding chair. Maybe I will read one of your stories in a book!

Fondly,

Maria LaPlaca Bohrer

You will need an adult's permission, supervision, and assistance in making Nana's delicious meatballs!

Nana's Meatballs

2 lbs. ground beef
5 slices of white bread (crumble and moisten with water)
2 cloves of garlic (chopped)
2 eggs (beat in a cup)
1 cup grated Romano cheese
¼ cup of chopped fresh Italian parsley
pinch of salt
pinch of pepper
½ cup of homemade tomato sauce
olive oil (to fry meatballs)

Place ground beef in a large bowl and make a well in center.
Add all ingredients (except olive oil) and mix.
Shape mixture into 2 inch balls and place on plate.
Heat oil. Carefully place meatballs in hot oil, turning them as they brown.
Carefully remove cooked meatballs. Place on a plate lined with paper towels.
Add meatballs to your favorite tomato sauce.

Mangia! Mangia!